The First Christmas

retold by LYNNE BRADBURY
illustrated by LYNN N GRUNDY

Ladybird Books

A long time ago Mary and Joseph had to leave their home in Nazareth and travel to Bethlehem.

The Christmas story is a perennial favourite and this delightfully simple version will appeal to all young listeners and early readers.

Titles in Series S846

The First Christmas

***Noah's Ark**

***Moses**

***Joseph**

***David**

***Daniel**

The Lord's Prayer

*These titles are available as a Gift Box set

First edition

Published by Ladybird Books Ltd Loughborough Leicestershire UK
Ladybird Books Inc Lewiston Maine 04240 USA

Printed in England

It was a long, hard journey and Mary rode on a donkey while Joseph walked beside her.

Mary was going to have a baby.
An angel had come to her and told her that she would have a baby boy and that she should name him Jesus.

Mary knew that her baby would be born soon.

By the time they reached Bethlehem, Mary and Joseph were very tired and they needed to find a place to sleep. But the town was full of people and everywhere they went they were told that there was no room for them.

Then one innkeeper saw how tired Joseph and Mary were, and he remembered that he had a stable which was warm and dry. He said that they could sleep there.

Joseph made a bed of hay for Mary.
The donkey and an ox watched over her.

That night Mary's baby was born.
They wrapped the baby Jesus in warm clothes and laid Him in a manger where hay had been put for the animals.

On a hillside near Bethlehem some shepherds were watching over their sheep through the night.

Suddenly there was a bright light and angels came to them. One angel said, ''Don't be afraid. Jesus has been born and you will find Him in a stable in Bethlehem.''

The shepherds were very happy at the good news and went to Bethlehem to find the stable.

When they got there they saw the baby Jesus lying in the manger. Joseph and Mary were watching over Him.

Far away in the East, a bright new star appeared in the sky.

Three Wise Men saw the star and they knew that it was to tell them that a new baby king had been born.

Night after night they rode on their camels and followed the star, until it finally stopped over the stable where Jesus had been born.

The three Wise Men went into the stable and saw their baby king.

They gave Him presents of gold, frankincense and myrrh before they left to go back to their own land.